W9-BFS-092

CAPTAIN
AWESOME
SAVES THE WINTER WONDERLAND

By STAN KIRBY   Illustrated by GEORGE O'CONNOR

LITTLE SIMON
New York   London   Toronto   Sydney   New Delhi

LITTLE SIMON

An imprint of Simon & Schuster Children's Publishing Division • 1230 Avenue of the Americas, New York, New York 10020 • Copyright © 2012 by Simon & Schuster, Inc. All rights reserved, including the right of reproduction in whole or in part in any form. LITTLE SIMON is a registered trademark of Simon & Schuster, Inc., and associated colophon is a trademark of Simon & Schuster, Inc. For information about special discounts for bulk purchases, please contact Simon & Schuster Special Sales at 1-866-506-1949 or business@simonandschuster.com. The Simon & Schuster Speakers Bureau can bring authors to your live event. For more information or to book an event contact the Simon & Schuster Speakers Bureau at 1-866-248-3049 or visit our website at www.simonspeakers.com. Manufactured in the United States of America 0812 FFG • First Edition 10 9 8 7 6 5 4 3 2 1

Library of Congress Cataloging-in-Publication Data

Kirby, Stan. Captain Awesome saves the winter wonderland / by Stan Kirby ; illustrated by George O'Connor. — 1st ed. p. cm. Summary: When second-grader Eugene McGillicudy is forced to be the star of the students' winter play, he relies on his superpowered alter ego to help him. [etc.] [1. Superheroes—Fiction. 2. Schools—Fiction. 3. Theater—Fiction.] I. O'Connor, George, ill. II. Title. PZ7.K633529Cah 2012 [Fic]—dc23 2011028700

ISBN 978-1-4424-4334-1 (pbk)

ISBN 978-1-4424-4335-8 (hc)

ISBN 978-1-4424-4336-5 (eBook)

Table of Contents

TING!
TINGGG!
TINGGGGG!

"I love to play the triangle!" Eugene McGillicudy yelled out in a very heroic voice. In Mrs. Randle's music class, Eugene always went for the triangle. "I like any musical instrument that's shaped like a slice of pizza!"

SHAKE!
SHAKE-SHAKE!

"Keep your triangle," said Eugene's best friend, Charlie Thomas Jones. "I like the maracas. I don't know what's inside, but I hope it's dried bugs."

SHAKE!

Every Thursday morning, Sunnyview Elementary School's music teacher, Mrs. Randle, passed out an assortment of xylophones, tambourines, recorders, cowbells, bongo drums, and more to all the second graders in her music room.

Eager students from different classes grabbed them like free chocolate, and sang and played under Mrs. Randle's waving baton.

"Cowbell!" cried Evan Mason as he grabbed one from the stack.

"I'm getting the tambourine!" yelled Meredith Mooney, dressed in pink, from the ribbons in her hair to the shoelaces in her pink shoes. She had secretly stuck pink tape on the tambourine to mark it her own.

Then Colin Boyle, who was from Mrs. Duncan's second-grade class, grabbed a set of bongo drums. **BAMMITY-BAM! BAM!**

He bammed them with the palms of his hands. "Nice," he said.

"Okay, class," Mrs. Randle said. "Let's get started."

"And a one, and a two, and a one, two, three, four," she called, swinging her baton like she was swatting at a lazy fly.

Eugene tinged and Charlie shook, because superheroes who step in front of danger aren't afraid to make as much crazy loud music as possible. Just like that time Super Dude fought his musical enemy, Trouble Clef, and knocked the musical scales right off his slide trombone.

KA-PUNCH!

What's that?

You've never heard of Super Dude? Really?! Have you never been to a comic book store? Do you not watch cartoons on television? Do you not have the limited edition Super Dude Wristwatch?

Super Dude was absolutely the great- est superhero ever— he was also the star of a number of comic books. Eugene had boxes of them under his bed. And in his

closet. And stacked in the corner. Following Super Dude's example, Eugene created his own costume and became . . .

TA-DA!

CAPTAIN AWESOME!

Along with his best friend, Charlie, also known as the super-hero Nacho Cheese Man, he formed the Sunnyview Superhero Squad to stop evil from eviling in Sunnyview.

This was good because Eugene and Charlie lived in Sunnyview and there was a surprising amount of eviling going on.

But so far, at least for today, Charlie and Eugene hadn't seen any bad guys at Sunnyview Elementary School—just the happy, loud sounds of a triangle and a set of maracas.

TING!

SHAKE!

TINGGG!

SHAKE-SHAKE!

"Can we please stop all that noise?" asked the awful My! Me! Mine! Mere-DITH Mooney. The pink ribbons in her hair were tied in perfect bows. Her pink bows were perfect like the grades she expected on her report card.

Meredith had a lot of rules and one of them was about noise. "Noise," she always said to Eugene, "is noisy. And I doubt there's anything more noisy than *you*."

I'll bet she thinks it'll wrinkle all that pink, Eugene thought.

"Mrs. Randle, I can't concentrate on my tambourine if Barfgene and Charlie Thomas Bonehead keep making those awful sounds."

SHAKE!

"Is she talking about us?" Charlie whispered to Eugene.

TING!

"Bad guys always complain about superheroes," Eugene whispered back. Meredith was not only the pink Mooney who complained about everything, but she was also Captain Awesome's archenemy, Little Miss Stinky Pinky!

"Little Miss Stinky Pinky's trying to stop our Anti-Evil Symphony!" Charlie said.

"Well, that's what *she* thinks!" Eugene replied. "No evil is going to knock the notes off our scales today!"

CHAPTER 2

Is It Super
Zombie
Dinosaurs?

By
Eugene

"**C**lass, I have a special announcement to make," Mrs. Randle said.

A special announcement? Eugene *loved* special announcements.

"It's something very special," she added.

Very special announcements are even better, Eugene thought.

"Is the school going to be

turned into a rocket ship and blast off for Altair's green sun where all of my friends can get superpowers?" Eugene asked hopefully.

"Ummm . . no . . . ," Mrs. Randle said.

"Is the school going to be turned into the new headquarters for the League of Superheroes for Justice?" Charlie asked.

Mrs. Randle shook her head. "Not quite, Charlie."

Then it must be something really, awesomely superly biggish! Eugene thought.

"I know!" he called out. "The school's going to be turned into a giant science lab that takes zombie dinosaurs and turns them into *super* zombie dinosaurs!"

But no, that wasn't right, either. "Before we go on winter break," Mrs. Randle said, "we'll be performing our holiday play: *The Winter Wonderland!*"

Eugene and Charlie looked at each other.

"I thought you said it was something very special?" Eugene asked.

"It *is* very special!" Mrs. Randle

replied. "It's going to be a wonder-land of winter." She was so excited it was like she was jumping out of her shoes.

"Don't worry, Mrs. Randle. I'll star in the play for you," Meredith volunteered.

"Everyone will get a chance to participate," Mrs. Randle said. "Tryouts are on Monday. There will be songs, music, dancing, holiday lights, everything you need to make a wonderland!"

Songs and performances . . . in front of an audience . . . at school . . . at night?! Eugene's mind was twirling. *Maybe this* is *better than super zombie dinosaurs.*

"There'll be three rehearsals after school," Mrs. Randle said. "You guys have to be ready for your big stage debuts."

"I'm ready right now!" Eugene said. "Listen!" He *TINGED* his triangle again as hard as he could.

"That's really great, Eugene."
Mrs. Randle's ears were ringing.
"But you can sign up for the tryouts
here." She pointed to the clipboard
on her desk.

SCAMPER!

PUSH!

SHOVE!

"Make way!"

"Me first!"

"Where's that pencil?"

Everyone rushed to the sign-up sheet to list the parts they wanted to try out for. Eugene and Charlie shot each other a look. They knew instantly where they wanted to be.

"Are you thinking what I'm thinking, Charlie?"

"You bet I am," he said.

"Snowflake Symphony!"

they said at the same time.

"We'll be able to see the whole auditorium!" Eugene said. "As Captain Awesome and Nacho Cheese Man, we can keep an eye out for Sunnyview's major villains."

"No evil badness will sabotage our holiday play!" Charlie said.

But badness was already in the room. Who were all these people blocking their way to the clipboard? This was not a classroom filled with happy children, this was really the Evil Student Mutant League!

And they were out to stop Captain Awesome and Nacho Cheese Man from joining the Snowflake Symphony! Well, not today!

"Step aside, Evil Student Mutants!" Captain Awesome said.

CHAPTER 3

Trying Tryouts

BY
Eugene

In!

On Monday, Eugene's audition was super.

"MI-TEE!" he yelled. "I'm in the Snowflake Symphony! As lead triangle! Look out, Winter Wonderland! My Triangle of Justice shall ring loud this day!"

TING! TING! TING!

"Cheesy-YO!" Charlie said. "I'm in, too! Mrs. Randle said I shook the maracas like the best maracas-shaker she'd ever seen!"

SHAKE-SHAKE-SHAKE!

Evan Mason was next for his audition. He did a very dramatic performance as a snowflake.

"Today, I am a snowflake," Evan said. "Watch as I fall gently from the sky, landing safely on the ground, as quiet as a whisper. *Then!*" His voice became more dramatic. "I'm scooped up by a snowplow, scraped into a pile of snow by the side of the road, and mashed into a giant snow fort. The end!"

Next, Sally Williams did her impression of Super Snowball, the world's greatest snow-powered superhero. "I am Super Snowball!" she yelled in a very heroic voice. "No evil shall escape from my slushy snowballs!"

Sally ran around the

music room throwing imaginary snowballs at invisible villains. "Slush attack! Your crime is no match for my anti-evil snowballs!"

Wow! Sally can really fight evil, Eugene thought.

But it was Mike Flinch who really impressed Eugene—and everyone else in the class—with his song.

"Snowman,
snowman,
wonderland.

In the snow
globe in my hand.

If I shake you left and right,

Will you be dizzy day and night?

Snowman, snowman, wonderland!"

BRAVO!

Everyone in the class applauded. Mrs. Randle rushed to Mike and shook his hand.

"I think we've found our lead," she said. "Class, Mike will star as the Sunnyview Snowman in *The Winter Wonderland!*"

HOORAY!

Everyone knew how important that role was. Ted Lee was last year's Sunnyview Snowman and he went on to play the Cactus King in the Spring Pageant! Mike had big shoes to fill.

"Way to go, Mike!" Eugene and Charlie cheered.

"Uh . . . I'd like to thank my

Uncle Lewis for teaching me everything I know about show tunes," Mike said. The only thing bigger than Mike's smile was the big, round white snowman head he'd be wearing as his snowman costume.

"Yeah, yeah, that's great, hooray and all for Mike,"Meredith said. "But let's get to the really big news. What star part do I get to play?"

Mrs. Randle flipped through the notes on her clipboard. "You get to play the Icy Icicle in the Frozen Chorus!"

"What?!" she yelled. "What?!" she repeated. "What?!" she said again. "The Icy Icicle is *not* the star! It's just an *icicle*! What kind of play stars an *icicle*?! None! I should be the star!"

The pink ribbons in Meredith's hair shook so

hard that one of them popped out. She stomped off to the girls' bathroom to repair her pinkness.

Charlie and Eugene smiled at each other. What a great day!

"*The Winter Wonderland* is only a few weeks away," Mrs. Randle said. "After-school practices will be on the next two Thursdays from three-thirty to five p.m. Please let your parents know and have them sign your permission slips."

YAY!

"No homework on Thursday nights!" Eugene cheered.

"Oh no," Mrs. Randle corrected. "You'll still have to do your homework, but *Winter Wonderland* practice will be fun!"

BOO! Still have to do homework?! How is that fun?! Eugene wondered.

Some fun it was, if the dreaded Homework Monster from Planet Textbook was still assigning evil assignments! Enough was enough! It was time for Captain Awesome and Nacho Cheese Man to fight against the Homework Monster's unfair Study Bombs.

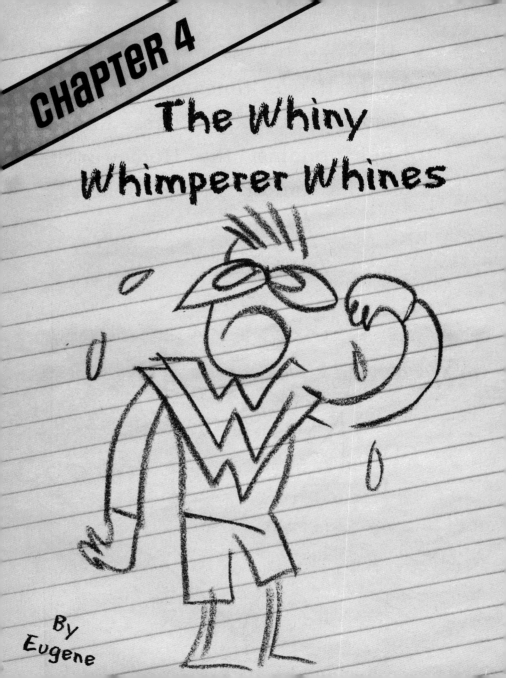

"I can see everything!" Eugene exclaimed, standing in the back row with the rest of the Snowflake Symphony.

"Do you have super vision too?" Charlie asked.

Eugene shook his head. "No, but I have the perfect seat to watch out for evil."

It was Thursday after school and all the *Winter Wonderland* performers arrived for their first rehearsal. While they stumbled around looking for their assigned seats, Eugene and Charlie were already sitting in theirs.

"It's good to get here early," Eugene said.

"Evil doesn't rest, even during rehearsals!" Charlie agreed.

"Evil doesn't stand a chance," Eugene said. "The citizens of Sunnyview have nothing to worry about with Captain Awesome and Nacho Cheese Man on the job."

TAP!
TAP!
TAP!

Eugene's anti-evil declarations were interrupted when Mrs. Randle tapped her baton against the music stand.

"Instruments...ready!"

she called out. "And a one, and a two, and a one, two, three, four!"

The Snowflake Symphony started to play the *Winter Wonderland* music. Eugene and Charlie played their instruments as loud as possible.

TING! TING! TING! SHAKE! SHAKE! SHAKE!

But then a hand shot up from the orchestra. "Mrs. Randle!" the hand called out.

Eugene traced the hand to Jake Story, a second-grader who was in Mrs. Martin's class. Jake stood up. He had red hair that was slicked back like bright red string. He was wearing a tie.

A TIE!

Who wears a tie to school? Eugene wondered.

And who keeps it on after school?

"Mrs. Randle, oh yoo-hoo! Mrs. Randle!" Jake called out.

"Yes, Jake?"

"I can't play *my* triangle because Eugene is banging on his way too loud," Jake said. "It's hurting my ears! And I *do* get ear infections . . ."

"Very well," Mrs. Randle said. "I have the perfect solution."

Mrs. Randle did have the perfect solution. For evil. She not only moved Eugene far away from Jake, but also from Charlie. Worse, Eugene's view of the audience was now blocked by branches from the giant snow-covered tree on the stage.

As Eugene grumbled in his new seat, he and Charlie shared a knowing look—the kind of all-knowing look that superheroes share whenever they realize there's a bad guy right in the room with them raising its evil hand and complaining about "ear infections."

This "Jake Story" from "Mrs. Martin's class" was clearly up to no good. For this was no ordinary second-grader! Jake was really **The Whiny Whimperer**, a

constant complainer determined to keep Captain Awesome and Nacho Cheese Man apart. If that was true, he was in for an awesome surprise!

But fear not! Captain Awesome and Nacho Cheese Man would not be separated by evil whining!

"**C**lass, I have a terrible announcement to make."

Oh no! Eugene thought. *Terrible announcements are always terrible!*

"Let me guess: Our principal is really an alien invader from the Planet Do-What-I-Tell-You?!" Eugene asked.

Mrs. Randle chuckled. "You have a wild imagination, Eugene, but alien invaders would be good news today."

If alien invaders were good news, what could possibly be the bad news?

Eugene looked around for evil, but his Captain Awesome Evil-Detection Powers detected nothing out of the ordinary. "But Mrs. Randle, everything is where it should be. No one's taken the glittery pinecones.

The fake snowflakes are still in their boxes and even the Sunnyview Snowman costume is on its hook."

How bad can it be?

BAD.

"It seems that poor Mike Flinch has gotten the flu and will no longer be able to be the Sunnyview Snowman in the play," Mrs. Randle sadly informed the students.

"Oh, my," Meredith said, very dramatically. "Poor Mike! Poor, poor

Mike! Whatever will we do without him!" She pressed the back of her hand to her forehead like she was going to faint. "Looks like you'll need the best actor remaining to play the snowman," Meredith said, trying her hardest to be the best actor.

"Oh, I know what we can do—" Eugene started to say.

"So do I, Eww-Gene, so do I," Meredith interrupted. "*The Winter Wonderland* needs someone to come in and save the day. The play needs someone who can be the Sunnyview Snowman and make the Winter Wonderland a true wonder of winter." She looked at Mrs. Randle with really big eyes, "Tell me, Mrs. Randle, who will play the Snowman now and save our Wonderland?"

BARF! Could anyone be more barfier than Meredith?

"Thank you, Meredith, for that very dramatic performance, but you are perfect for the Icy Icicle."

"But I only have *one* line, Mrs. Randle!" Meredith protested. "'Brrrr . . . it's cold even for an icicle like me.' I could say it in my sleep."

"And you say it so well, dear," Mrs. Randle said. "Besides, after careful consideration, I've made my choice. The student playing the Sunnyview Snowman will be . . . **Eugene McGillicudy!**"

Mrs. Randle announced.

Poor kid, Eugene thought, looking around to see if he could spot the miserable expression on the doomed student's face. *Stuck looking like he's wearing a white bowling ball on his head while he sings with Meredith Moo— BY THE BARF IN MY MOUTH! EUGENE MCGILLICUDY?! THAT'S ME!*

"Aaaaaaaaaaaaaaaaaaaaaaah! I don't want to wear a white bowling ball on my head!"

"Oh, Eugene!" Mrs. Randle replied. "The snowman's head isn't a white bowling ball. It's a white *plastic* ball . . . with holes for eyes." She snapped the large, white ball on Eugene's head.

"You look like you're wearing a marshmallow helmet," Charlie whispered. "Like Marshy the Evil

Marshmallow King from Super Dude No. 56."

"Come on, Eugene. You're in the front row, now. Right next to Meredith."

The walk from the back row to the front row, where he would be beside a fuming icicle in pink ribbons, was only fifteen feet, but to Eugene it felt like he was walking a billion miles with a marshmallow helmet on his head.

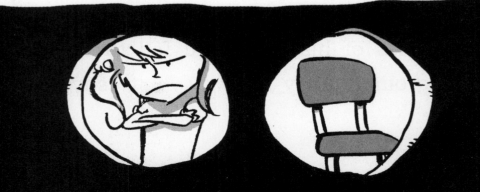

Eugene slid in next to Meredith. He had to get out of the front row. *I'll never be able to see any villains from here!*

Eugene knew he couldn't tell Mrs. Randle the truth. He couldn't let anyone know he was really Captain Awesome. So he came up with the next best excuse.

"Mrs. Randle! The marshmallow helmet has brain-sucking eels inside! They're sucking out my braaaaaains!" Eugene grabbed the sides of his head and fell to the ground. "Only . . . way . . . to save me . . . is to move me . . . into the . . . back row . . . again."

Mrs. Randle stared at Eugene, slightly annoyed. "Eugene. It's *not* a marshmallow helmet. It's the head of the Sunnyview Snowman, but if you think you can do a better job, then you can make the snowman's costume next year."

"Braaaaaaaains . . ." Eugene gurgled and squirmed on the floor.

"I think someone is just acting out because they're nervous about being the snowman . . . ," Mrs. Randle said.

"I'd be nervous, too, if I danced like Eubean." Meredith snorted.

"Let's make a promise to each other, Eugene." Mrs. Randle helped him up from the floor. "I promise that I'll help you to be a GREAT snowman. And you promise me that you'll stop ruining my costumes."

Eugene felt the side of his

head. Rolling around had dented the side of the Styrofoam helmet. *Great. Now I'm going to be a block-head snowman.*

Eugene sighed. There was no way out. He would have to sing and dance with an angry pink Popsicle, and Charlie would have to be on villain patrol alone.

"Deal," Eugene finally replied, knowing exactly how Super Dude felt when he had to disguise himself as a turnip to save the Cauliflower Kid from the steamy Cabbage Patch in Super Dude No. 12 *Special Vegetarian Edition.*

"Okay, my little snowflakes and icicles and snowmen and all you other wintry things, let's try the play's dance finale, 'Jingle Bells'!" Mrs. Randle called out.

"Dashing through the snow, in a one course soapy day!" Eugene's warbly voice warbled while he counted "One, two, three" in his head to keep his dancing feet in

time with Meredith's. But when
Meredith spun left, Eugene spun
right and . . .

Eugene crashed into Philip Fernbottom who was dressed as a winter pinecone. Then Philip stumbled and fell into Sonia DeRosa, a snow-flake, who bumped into Charlie and caused the whole row of snowflakes

to topple like white, glittery dominoes.

The music stopped as kids in various winter costumes rolled on their backs and waved their arms like overturned turtles.

"I don't even know where to

start," Meredith started. "*First* of all, what does 'One course soapy day' even mean?"

"How should I know?" Eugene defended. "I didn't write the song."

"It's 'One *horse open sleigh*,' Eubean," Meredith corrected. "And you spun right when you were supposed to spin left. You *do* know the difference between left and right, right?"

"*Yeah*," Eugene replied. He stood silently with his arms crossed, but then realized everyone was staring. "Left! See!" he snapped,

raising his left hand.

"That'll show her!" Charlie whispered, waddling on the ground near Eugene's feet, waiting for someone to help him stand up.

CHAPTER 6

Chilly with a Slight Chance of Evil!

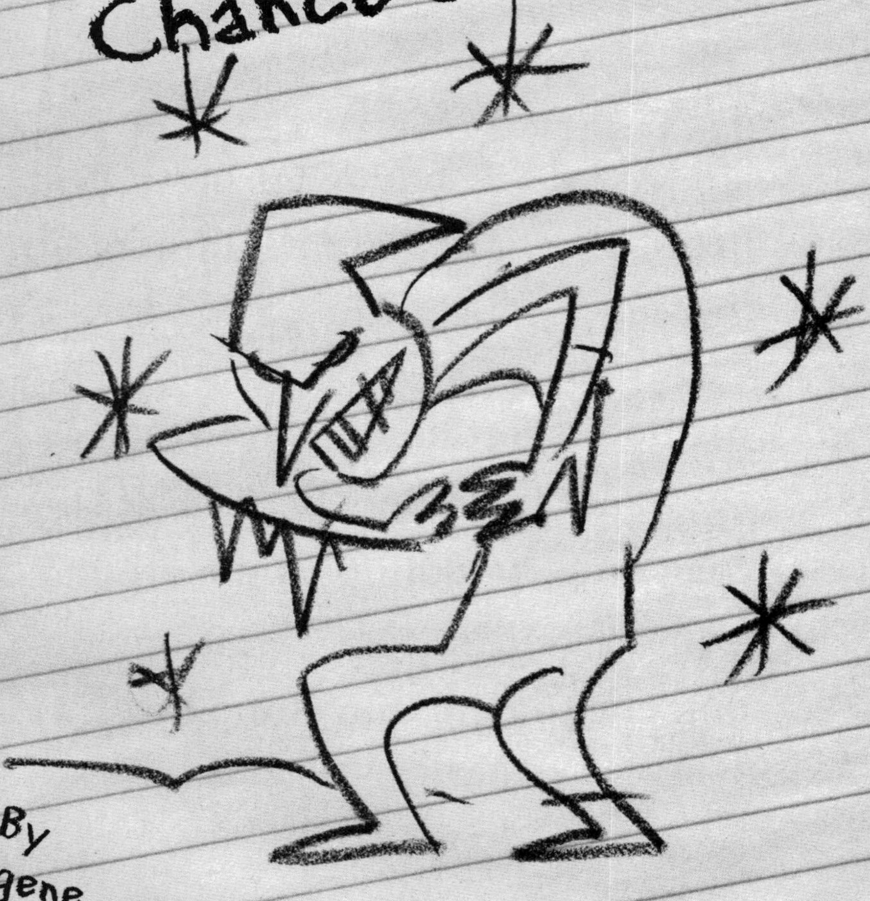

By Eugene

"Any play rehearsal that ends with Meredith mad at you can't be all that bad," Charlie offered as the two boys walked home after school.

Eugene felt happy to be out of the snow-man costume.

"I don't know why Mrs. Randle picked me to be the snowman," Eugene sighed, small white sparkles falling from his ear. "I can't sing or dance and the snowman is the most important part of the play!"

"I know! I don't know what Mrs. Randle was thinking!" Charlie laughed until he saw Eugene glaring at him. "I mean . . . I don't know what Mrs. Randle was thinking . . . when she . . . made that snowman costume."

"And the worst part is, I have to dance with My! Me! Mine! Mere-DITH!" Eugene groaned. "Oh, Charlie, why would Mrs. Randle do this to me?"

A light went off in Charlie's head. "That's it! There's no better place to watch for the bad guys than center stage!"

"You're right!" Eugene replied. "I'll bet Mrs. Randle is a double undercover secret spy sent to help us defeat the evil bad stuff that evil does!"

"This calls for a Double Nacho Cheese Celebration!" Charlie cheered. He slid off his backpack and pulled out a can of nacho cheese.

EMPTY!

"Cheesy underwear! I'm out!" Charlie said in disbelief. "Do you have my backup can?"

"Don't I always?" Eugene reached inside his backpack, but something besides Charlie's canned cheese awaited within.

"It's a note . . ." Eugene showed the crayon-scrawled paper to Charlie.

"'Ice to meet you. My name is Mr. Chill,'" Charlie read, his eyes wide. "'If you had cold feet at the rehearsal today, you'll really get the

big freeze tomorrow if
you don't quit the play. Catch
my *drift*? PS This is snow joke.'"

"Someone wants me to quit the
play? But who?" Eugene asked.

"I'll bet it was Meredith!"
Charlie gasped.

"Impossible!" Eugene said, studying the note. "Her writing is way nicer than this and she'd have little hearts and butterflies and pink unicorns with wings drawn all over it."

Both boys stood in silence imagining the horrors of an evil note threatening to put the "big freeze"on Eugene, covered in hearts and butterflies and pink unicorns with wings.

"That's just gross," Charlie said.

CHAPTER 7

The Return of
Mr. Chill

By
Eugene

Time passed. Hours turned into days and days turned into more days. Eugene practiced every day. He sang. He danced. He counted in his head. And then a very strange thing happened.

"Oh, what fun, it is to ride, in a one . . . horse . . . o-pen sleiiiiiiigh!"

Eugene sang the song perfectly. He didn't knock down a single winter pinecone or snowflake *or* the

angry, pink Icicle. He raised his little snowman arms into the air and belted out the last words of "Jingle Bells."

Mrs. Randle was right. He *could* do this.

As the song ended, Eugene the Snowman stood perfectly still. The snowflakes of Sunnyview gathered around him and carefully placed decorations on his snowman costume.

"And as the snowflakes place the decorations on you, *that's* when you say the last line of the play, "'Snow glad you could all come. Happy holidays!'" Mrs. Randle said.

But Eugene wasn't listening. He was doing something much more important. His eyes scanned the faces of his fellow *Winter Wonderland* performers.

Who wrote that note? he wondered. *Which one of you wants me out of the play?*

Meredith as the angry Icicle was the last one to place a decoration on Eugene with a big, fat YAWN!

"That was wonderful! Simply wonderful!" Mrs. Randle gushed. "And Eugene ... you were marvelous."

Eugene didn't reply. His cheeks turned red, and he stared at the ground.

"But Meredith, my dear . . ."
Mrs. Randle continued, "the end is
supposed to be a celebration. You
looked so . . . bored."

"Don't you worry," grumpy
Meredith said to Mrs. Randle.
"When that curtain rises on open-
ing night, I'll bring it."

As Mrs. Randle continued
giving tips to the rest of the students, Eugene gave a thumbs-up to
Charlie.

SNEAK!

ZIP!

SUPERHERO!

Within seconds,
the boys were backstage digging
their superhero outfits from their
backpacks.

"Over here!" Captain Awesome
whispered.

Nacho Cheese Man grabbed
a can of hot dog–flavored cheese
and crept with Captain Awesome

behind a large dressing mirror.

"We can hide back here and watch my backpack!" Captain Awesome explained in an awesome, yet still very whispery voice.

And then—as Nacho Cheese Man took the first suck of flavored canned cheese—THEY SAW IT!

A HAND!

WITH A NOTE!

REACHING FOR EUGENE'S BACKPACK!

"Mun mand mat matmack!" Nacho Cheese Man leapt from behind the large mirror and shouted, his tongue sticking to the roof of his mouth.

"Freeze or face Captain Awesome's One–Two Spinning Punch!" Captain Awesome called out. He spun around and around, his arms extended like blades of a helicopter.

The hand dropped the note! Running footsteps echoed!

Captain Awesome spun in two more circles, staggered forward and tripped over his backpack.

"Whoa . . . dizzy . . . too much whirlwinding . . ."

"Mall met mim!" Nacho Cheese Man said, trying desperately to unstick his tongue from the roof of his mouth.

Then, something moved! The heroes spun and faced a walking pinecone!

"AAAAAAAAAH!" they both screamed before realizing it was just Philip Fernbottom.

"Whoa," Philip said. "Are you guys in the play?"

"Yes! In the 'play' of Good versus Evil!" Captain Awesome replied. "But there's no singing *or* dancing. There's

only the crushing of evil beneath my Superhero Sneakers."

Philip Fernbottom took one look at himself dressed as a giant pinecone and said, "I wanna be in *your* play."

But it was too late. Captain Awesome and Nacho Cheese Man were gone. Into the back wings of the stage they raced! Something moved again! This time it wasn't a pinecone. Someone was behind the giant cardboard candy cane leaning against the wall . . . and it sure wasn't one of Santa's elves.

Nacho Cheese Man ran to the other side of the candy cane, cutting off all hope of escape for the cowering bad guy.

"Show your face, if you dare!" Captain Awesome said.

A boy stood up from behind the candy cane prop.

"The Whiney Whimperer?!" Captain Awesome and Nacho Cheese Man gasped in unison.

"Why can't you call me 'Mr. Chill?'" Jake Story whined.

"I don't like being called 'The Whiney Whimperer.'"

"Sorry, villain, but *we* get to name the bad guys, not you," Captain Awesome replied. "That's just what goodness does!"

"And the other thing goodness does is to find out who you're working for!" Nacho Cheese Man called out as the two heroes rushed into action!

"CHEESY-YO!" "MI-TEE!"

CHAPTER 8

Jake and the Stampeding Elephant

By Eugene

"I only wanted Eugene to quit the play so I could be the star," Jake confessed. His red, greased-back hair made it look like he had orange jam smeared all over his head. *"I'm* a better triangle player than he is *and* a better dancer! Watch!"

Jake danced. Sort of. He looked more like a puppet flopping about after some of his strings had been cut. He did a final spin and crashed into Nacho Cheese Man.

"Okay, so, maybe I need to work on that part a little bit more, but I'm still a better triangle player!" Jake whined.

"The only thing you're better at is making my ears hurt," Captain Awesome replied. "Now, who else is in on your chilly plan of evil?!"

"Yeah! Who *are* you with?!" Nacho Cheese Man snapped. "I'll bet it's Dr. Spinach! Or Queen Stinkypants!"

"No one! I don't even know who Queen Spinach and Dr. Stinkypants are! Honest!" Jake claimed. "I was just tired of Eugene getting all the attention. It's just like at home. No one *ever* pays attention to me."

With all that bright red hair on Jake's head, Captain Awesome found it hard to believe at first, but then he thought about the times that his own parents hovered over Molly and he felt totally forgotten.

He could be playing a trumpet on the back of a stampeding elephant crashing cymbals with its trunk and the only reaction his parents would have would be "Oooo! Molly just made a stinky in

her diaper! Who's our little stinky stinkpot?"

Captain Awesome knew that his parents would never, ever really forget him, but sometimes that's still how he *felt*.

Sometimes.

"Please don't tell Mrs. Randle!" Jake pleaded. "I don't want to be kicked out of the play!"

"Don't worry, Jake," Captain Awesome said, calling the boy by his real name. "Your secret is safe with Captain Awesome and Nacho Cheese Man."

"Yeah! And that's what you get for going up against Captain Awesome and—" Nacho Cheese Man threw a confused look to Captain Awesome. "Wait. Did you just say 'your secret is safe?'"

"Yes, Nacho Cheese Man. Safe. If there's one thing Super Dude taught us, it's that sometimes you gotta kick evil in the butt, sometimes you gotta punch evil in the face, but sometimes what you really need to do is . . . help. Like Super Dude says, it's the job of a true hero to know the difference."

"Cheesy-yo . . . ," Nacho Cheese Man whispered in a voice mixed with wonder and admiration. "And that's one more reason why they call him '*Super* Dude . . .'"

Captain Awesome turned from his crime-fighting friend and extended his hand to Jake.

"I think I'm gonna puke!" Eugene groaned.

Charlie took a big step to the left. "You'll be fine," he said, then took another step away just to be safe.

"But everyone in the world is out there!" Eugene replied. He peeked through the curtain to see the school auditorium packed with parents and families.

"It's opening night! How's my little snowman doing?" Mrs. Randle asked.

"I think I'm gonna puke!" Eugene groaned.

Mrs. Randle took a big step to the left. "You'll be fine," she said, then took another step away just to be safe.

It was finally the night of the play! The curtain rose to thunderous applause. The snowflakes shuffled out to the main stage.

"Go get 'em!" Jake whispered to Eugene as he passed.

Charlie added, "You'll do great!"

The music started. Eugene waited in the wings for his cue.

GURGLE!

His stomach was going on a roller-coaster ride around his heart.

LOOP!

Then it was in his nose.

ZOOM!

Then it took a twisting turn down to his knees.

And then, just as Eugene's stomach was rocketing down to his ankles, he caught a glimpse of himself in the dressing mirror.

He wasn't just wearing a giant marshmallow suit with a bright red scarf. He was wearing a *costume*. Yes, he looked like a little cloud with sneakers float-ing behind a red curtain, but it was still a costume he was wearing . . .

Just like my Captain Awesome outfit . . . , Eugene realized.

And suddenly his stomach's wild ride slowed down just a little bit. Then as Eugene calmed, a horrible "waaah!" of horribleness filled his ears!

"WAAAAAH!" a voice cried out from the audience.

I'd know that waaahing waaah waah anywhere! Eugene thought and yanked back the curtain.

And there she was! His most

stinky of enemies!

QUEEN STINKYPANTS!

But what was she doing *here*?! *Maybe she just wants to see me sing and dance,* Eugene wondered. *Even villains have been known to enjoy a nice winter play. . . .*

What am I thinking?! Eugene said to himself. *My snowman helmet must be on too tight! Queen Stinkypants can only be here for one reason . . . TO MAKE SURE THIS PLAY STINKS!*

But there was no time to change into his Captain Awesome

outfit. Eugene had to stop Queen Stinkypants from ruining the play! Every parent had one arm in the air, recording their kids with their smartphones. A hundred childhood memories would be forever ruined by the stinky stink of Stinkypants!

"The show must go on!" Eugene the Snowman shouted and rushed onto the stage!

CHEERS!
APPLAUSE!
HOORAY!

The play was perfect, filled with laughs, smiles and 152 individual smartphone cameras. And the strangest thing? It was all a blur for Eugene. His snowman instincts took over, and he danced and sang like he'd been doing the same thing every night for his entire life.

Even Meredith the Icy Icicle did a great job. When she told Mrs. Randle not to worry about her once the curtain went up, she wasn't kidding.

Eugene the Snowman and Meredith the Icicle went into the final moves of their dance. Eugene raised his arms and the snow-flakes gathered round with their decorations.

And then an idea came to Eugene. He stepped forward from the group and looked directly at the audience. Time for the last line

of the play. All the smartphones focused on Eugene, except for the one being held by Meredith's mom. Meredith had given her a strict *no-close-ups-on-anyone-but-me* order, and Mrs. Mooney was not about to break it.

"Thank you for coming," Eugene began, "But no Sunnyview celebration would be complete without a word from a very special snowflake . . ."

The auditorium was completely silent except for the ruffling of pages as Mrs. Randle stood in the wings desperately searching through the script to find the lines Eugene was saying.

Eugene coughed. Nothing. Charlie coughed. Nothing. Eugene and Charlie coughed again together. Still nothing. Meredith rolled her eyes, half annoyed and half afraid the two boys would point at her and start shouting their usual "nonsense" about Ms. Pinky

Stinky or Dinky Pinky or whatever it was they always called her.

"Are you okay?" Jake whispered to Eugene.

"Dude, I'm talking about *you*," Eugene whispered back. "Go on . . . say the last line . . . "

Jake paused for a moment, unsure he was hearing Eugene correctly.

He was.

The only thing bigger than Jake's eyes was his smile. He stepped forward into the spotlight. Every smartphone in the audience focused on Jake. Even Mrs. Mooney "accidentally"(as she would explain to her very grumpy daughter hours later when Meredith watched the video at home) zoomed in ever-so-slightly on Jake.

"Snow glad you could all come," he said. "Happy holidays!"

Applause exploded from the audience as everyone stood to cheer Jake and all the performers ... and no one cheered louder than the first row, filled with two red-headed parents and six red-headed brothers and sisters, who at that moment, were very much paying total attention to their son and brother.

MI-TEE!

"Sometimes, what you really need to do is help," Charlie the Snowflake whispered to Eugene the Snowman.

"That is snow true, Charlie," Eugene answered. "Snow true . . ."

IF YOU LIKE
CAPTAIN AWESOME,
YOU'LL LOVE

GALAXY ZACK

HERE'S A SNEAK PEEK!

"You'll love it on Nebulon, Captain," Dad said. "Wait'll you see the gadgets they have there. They're way ahead of Earth!"

"That sounds pretty cool," Zack said. Then he grew quiet. *Dad's got his great new job at Nebulonics, Zack thought. Mom wants to start her own business. And the twins always have each other. They don't have to worry about making new friends.*

Zack leaned back in his seat and closed his eyes.

"Okay, class, time for our Zerbanese language lesson," said someone with a strange, high-pitched voice.

Zack's eyes popped open. He was in a classroom on Nebulon. All his classmates looked like monsters. And slimy creatures with dripping tentacles sat all around him. The teacher looked like a giant two-headed snake.

Zack dashed from the classroom and ran across the street. He hurried toward a huge sign that flashed the words: THIS GALAXY'S BEST PIZZA.

Zack loved pizza. "Ah, pizza," he said. It was his favorite food. "At least they have *something* I know on this wacky, crazy planet!"

Zack rushed into the pizza place and ordered a whole pie. "I'll have today's special pizza, please."

Soon a steaming pizza floated down from above.

"YAAA!" yelled Zack. The pizza

was covered with slithering worms and crawling insects. It was topped with extra-moldy cheese.

Zack screamed and ran from the pizza place. He pulled out his video-chat hyperphone. Then he quickly entered Bert's z-mail address.

"Gotta talk to Bert," Zack mumbled to himself. "Maybe he can help me."

The screen on the hyperphone blinked. Then a message popped up: "ERROR . . . CANNOT CONNECT TO EARTH."

"I'm trapped here! And I'll never see or talk to my friends again!"